# A Christmas Present for Barney Bunny

Maria Cleary

Illustrated by Lorenzo Sabbatini

# Play Station 1

## 1 Listen and point.

## 2 Listen, colour and write.

Barney is wearing
a red ................................,
a yellow ................................,
a green ................................,
brown ................................,
orange ................................,
and blue ................................

boots
coat
gloves
hat
scarf
trousers

## 3 Listen and write the names.

| Billy | Betsey | Becky | Barney | Benjy |
|---|---|---|---|---|

## 4 Circle the words.

BOOTSGLOVESTROUSERSSCARFHATDRESSCOATSKIRT

# Play Station 1

**5** **Read and match.**

**6** **Listen. Say the chant.**

Let's play chase!
Run, run, run!
Let's play skipping!
Fun, fun, fun!
Let's play hopscotch!
Hop, hop, hop!
Let's play leapfrog!
Up, up, up!
Hide and seek, hide and seek,
let's play together all the week!

## 7 Listen and tick (✔).

| | ☺ | ☹ |
|---|---|---|
| chase | | |
| hide and seek | | |
| hopscotch | | |
| leapfrog | | |
| skipping | | |

## 8 Talk to a friend.

Betsey likes ..........................................

Betsey doesn't like ..........................................

## 9 What do you like? Draw and write.

I like ..........................................

..........................................................

..........................................................

..........................................................

..........................................................

..........................................................

..........................................................

..........................................................

..........................................................

It's Christmas Eve.
Mother Bunny is very busy.
She's making the dinner
and wrapping the presents
and tidying the house.

The little bunnies aren't
helping her.
They're shouting
and fighting
and making a mess.

Point to the bunnies.
Barney is helping.
Benjy and Betsey are running and shouting.
Billy and Becky are fighting.

“Stop shouting and fighting and making a mess!” says Mother Bunny.
“And go outside and play!”

“Where’s my hat?” says Benjy.
“Where’s my coat?” says Becky.
“You’ve got my gloves,” says Billy.
“And you’ve got my boots,” says Betsey.
“I can’t find my hat, or my coat, or my gloves, or my boots or my scarf,” says Barney, the baby bunny.

I don't like chase!
Where is Becky?
She is in front of .......................... .............. and behind .......................... .............. .

Now the bunnies are all outside.
"Let's play chase," says Benjy.
The bunnies are very fast.
Barney can't catch them.
"I don't like chase," he says.

"Let's play hopscotch," says Becky.
"Look there's a stone," says Betsey.
"We can draw with it."

All the bunnies can hop.
All the bunnies except Barney.
"I don't like hopscotch,"
says Barney.

"Let's play skipping," says Betsey.
"There's an old rope."
Benjy and Billy are turning the rope.
And Becky and Betsey are skipping.
Barney is watching. He can't skip.

"I don't like skipping,"
says Barney.

Write your best friend's name in the skipping chant.

I like coffee, I like tea.

I like .................................................... to skip with me.

“Let’s play leapfrog,” says Billy.

First it’s Billy’s turn.
He can jump very high.
Then it’s Barney’s turn.
Barney is small.
And Benjy, Betsey, Becky and Billy are tall.
He can’t jump over them.

"I don't like leapfrog," says Barney.
I don't like leapfrog!
Barney is small. What about you? Measure your height with a friend.
I'm .................................... cm.

“Let’s play hide and seek,” says Barney.
“1 – 2 – 3 – 4 – 5 – 6. . .” Benjy is counting.

Betsey is hiding behind the tree.
Billy is hiding under the wheelbarrow.
Becky is hiding on the branch.
And Barney...
Where is Barney hiding?

Say the numbers from 1 to 10.

Then say the numbers from 10 to 1.

How fast are you?

Barney is hiding in the shed.
It's very dark.
And Barney doesn't like the dark.

Oh dear! It's dark outside, too!
And the bunnies are not there.
Barney is very afraid.

What colours are the paints?

Say the colours with a friend.

Suddenly there is a light in the distance.
It's Mother Bunny.
And all the other bunnies are beside her.

"Barney, come! It's time for dinner,"
says Mother Bunny.
Barney runs to Mother.
He's safe!

The next day there are Christmas presents for all the little bunnies. There are running shoes for Benjy, and coloured chalks for Becky. There's a new skipping rope for Betsey and a soft green frog for Billie.

“And this is for you, Barney,”
says Mother Bunny.
“A bright torch. Now you can
see in the dark.”

# Play Station 2

**1 Look, read and put the story in order.**

"Let's play hide and seek," says Barney.

Barney is hiding in the shed. He is afraid.

"Go outside and play," says Mother Bunny.

"It's cold. Let's play chase," says Benjy.

There is Mother Bunny. Barney is safe.

Mother Bunny is very busy. The little bunnies aren't helping her.

**2 Look and tell the story to a friend.**

## 3 Read and tick (✓) Yes or No.

| | | YES | NO |
|---|---|---|---|
| A | The bunnies are helping Mother Bunny. | | |
| B | Barney can't find his clothes. | | |
| C | It's cold outside. | | |
| D | Barney is very fast. | | |
| E | Barney doesn't like skipping. | | |
| F | Billy can jump very high. | | |
| G | Barney is hiding behind the tree. | | |
| H | Mother Bunny has got a light. | | |

## 4 Find 17 words from the story (→↓).

**What do the remaining letters spell?**

_ _ _ _ _   _ _ _ _ _ _ _ _ _ _ _ !

# Play Station 2

**5** **Look and complete with the verbs.**

| fighting | making a mess | making the dinner | shouting | tidying the house | wrapping the presents |
|---|---|---|---|---|---|

A Mother Bunny is ............................................................ .

B Mother Bunny is ............................................................ .

C Mother Bunny is ............................................................ .

D The little bunnies are ................................................... .

E The little bunnies are ................................................... .

F The little bunnies are ................................................... .

**6** **Listen and check.**

## 7 Listen and match.

- They are running.
- They are skipping.
- She is wrapping presents.
- She is jumping.
- She is hiding.
- He is counting.

## 8 Listen and mime.

# Play Station 2

## 9 Read and match.

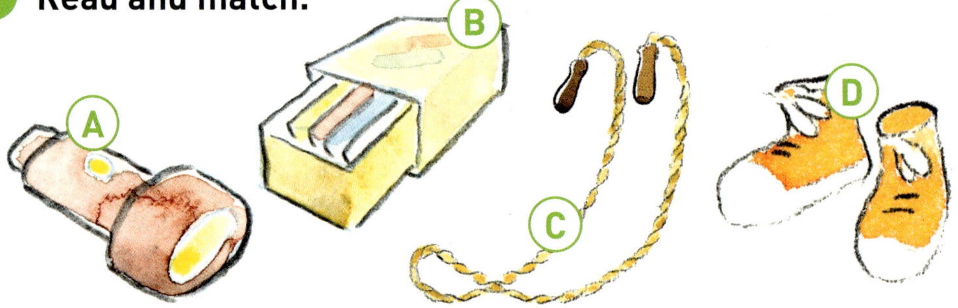


- ◯ You can skip with this.
- ◯ You can run fast with these.
- ◯ You can draw with these.
- ◯ You can see in the dark with this.

## 10 Read and draw a present for Mother Bunny.

## 11 Read and match.

- ◯ He's got a soft green frog.
- ◯ She's got a box of coloured chalks.
- ◯ She's got a skipping rope.
- ◯ He's got a bright torch.
- ◯ He's got running shoes.

## 12 Listen and circle the correct answer.

**A** Yes, he has. / No, he hasn't.

**B** Yes, she has. / No, she hasn't.

**C** Yes, he has. / No, he hasn't.

**D** Yes, he has. / No, he hasn't.

**E** Yes, she has. / No, she hasn't.

# Play Station Project

## Christmas Tree

**Make a Christmas tree for your class.**

**You need:**

lots of green paper
1 sheet of brown paper
1 sheet of yellow paper
1 large sheet of card
scissors
glue

1. Draw your hand on green paper. Cut out the hand print.

2. Write a Christmas greeting on your print.
   - Happy Christmas
   - Best Wishes
   - Merry Christmas

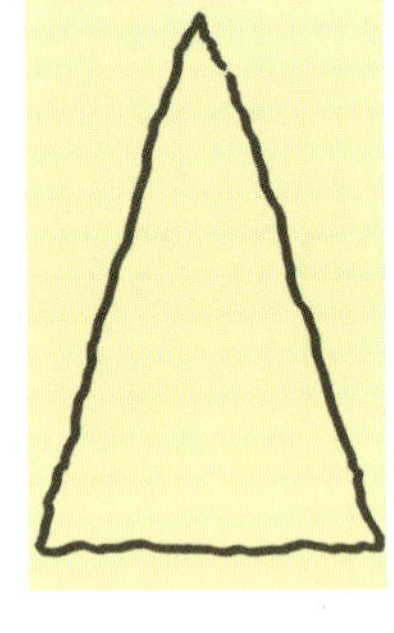

3. Draw a triangle on the sheet of card.

4. Cut a rectangle of brown paper. Glue it under the triangle.

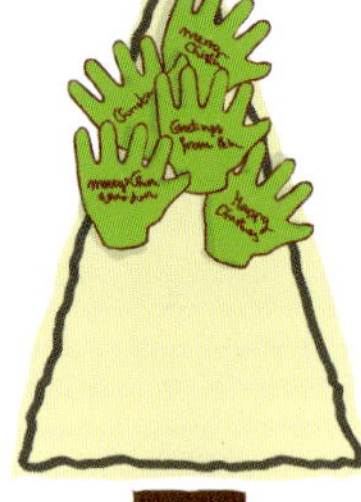

5. Glue the hand prints onto the tree.

6. Draw a star on the yellow paper. Cut it out and glue it onto the top of the tree.

Go to www.helblingyoungreaders.com to download this page.